The Poodle in the Puddle

SUSAN MARKS WEINER

Illustrated By Dwight Nacaytuna

ISBN: Softcover 978-1-5035-8856-1
EBook 978-1-5035-8857-8

Print information available on the last page

Rev. date: 07/27/2015

To order additional copies of this book, contact:
Xlibris
1-888-795-4274
www.Xlibris.com
Orders@Xlibris.com

Dedication

This book is dedicated to Mark and Jordan for their encouragement and to Sammie and Polo, my inspiration.

Sammie was walking home from school in the pouring rain. She was wearing her slicker and galoshes, jumping through the pools of water making splishes and sploshes when what did she see but a poodle in a puddle. He was just a little dog sitting in a muddy bog. He was shivering and quivering, whimpering and whining. Sammie felt sorry for him. He was so wet and cold. She thought to herself, "I will take poodle home and daddy will know what to do."

She took off her slicker and wrapped up the pup, put him in her arms and ran to her house as fast as she could. At the door, daddy was surprised at seeing the muddy wet poodle. "What is this, he exclaimed? Where did you find this dog?" Sammie said, "He is the poodle in the puddle, cold and wet! He needs help to get warm and dry... and he is hungry too I'll bet."

Daddy said, "Let's clean him up and dry him off. When he is warm and dry we can give him something to eat. Then we can try and find where he lives." Daddy took the dog to the tub with Sammie in tow.

And while daddy gave the poodle a bath Sammie was daydreaming. "What do poodles eat she wondered? Do poodles eat noodles or snicker doodles? Do they eat fishes or grandmom's knishes, tomatoes, potatoes, pie or chocolate cookies? What about pancakes, strawberry milk or pizza, hot dogs, or French Fries, cereal or pita?"

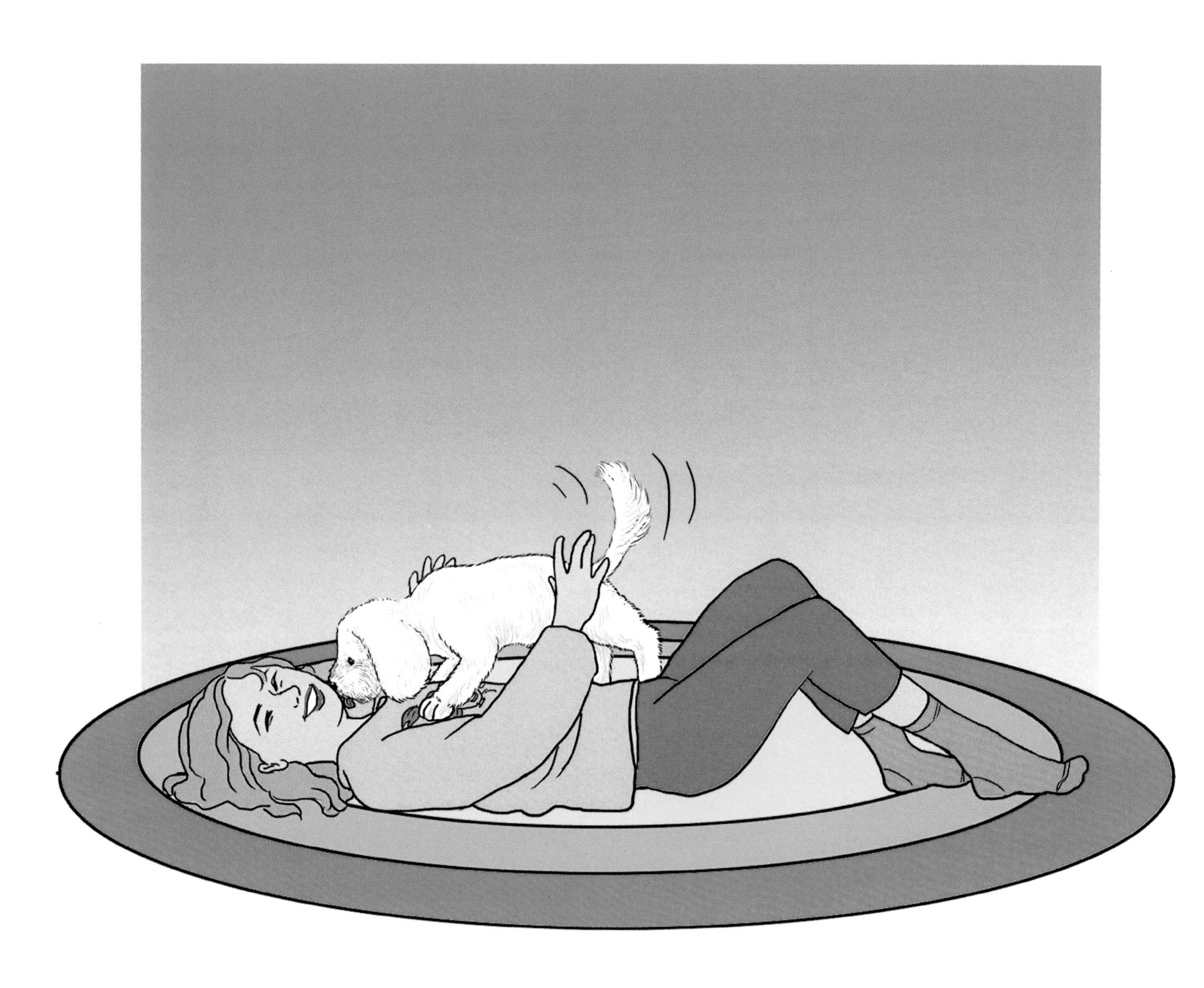

Sammie had no idea. The poodle was clean and daddy was wiping him off with a towel when he jumped up on Sammie knocking her down. Sammie was giggling and squirming while the poodle was licking her face and wagging his tail. Daddy said, "He is happy and thanking you for rescuing him. When a dog wags his tail it means he is happy and a dog lick is a kiss to you."

Just then mommy came home and saw the poodle. "What is this dog doing here?" she asked. Daddy and Sammie explained what had happened and mommy said, "It is important that we find where this dear little dog belongs. Someone is very sad because their pet is missing."

Supermarket
H647 KPE

Sammie said to mommy, "What do poodles eat?" Daddy replied, "Dog food and we have none so let's go to the store and get some." By then it had stopped raining. They all got in the car and went to the market. When they arrived, daddy asked mommy to stay in the car with Sammie and the poodle while he went to buy some dog food.

When they returned home daddy fed the poodle. "Boy, was he hungry!" said Sammie as she watched him lick the bowl clean. Mommy said, "Tomorrow we will try to find out who this little pup belongs to and get him home." Sammie wanted to keep him but she knew some other boy or girl was sad because he was lost.

At bedtime Sammie got into bed and the poodle laid down on the carpet beside her. "Good night, poodle," she said and they both fell asleep. In the morning, Sammie was getting ready to go to school. Poodle was following Sammie wherever she went in the house.

At breakfast mommy showed Sammie the signs she had made to try and find the dog's owners. The sign said 'Poodle dog found yesterday, please call this phone number' and Sammie saw her house phone number at the bottom of the paper. Sammie wondered if the poodle was sad that he was lost but happy that she and mommy and daddy were helping him find his home. "What do poodles need?" she asked her mommy and daddy. Daddy said, "Poodles need oodles of love and care, a warm house to live in and someone to brush their hair." Mommy added, "They also need to be walked and fed, someone to play with and a nice warm bed."

On the way to school daddy and Sammie put the signs up in the supermarket, the bakery, and the post office. Sammie said to daddy when she got out of the car to walk into school, "I feel glad that we found the poodle but sad that someone will come take him away." "That is an okay way to feel," said daddy. "That is called feeling 'conflicted' which means wanting to do the right thing but feeling sad because you are doing it. Don't worry, maybe the boy or girl who the poodle belongs to will let you see him from time to time."

When Sammie got home from school there was a strange car in the driveway and when she went into the house the poodle came running to the door to greet her and right behind the poodle was a little girl.

"Hi, I'm Lin and this is my dog, Polo. I am sooo glad to see him. I was afraid something bad had happened to him. I was walking him in the rain yesterday and his collar came loose. He thought he was playing a trick on me by running away and splashing in the puddles. Then I fell chasing after him and got all wet and when I got up I had lost him." Just then Lin's mother came out of the kitchen with Sammie's mother. "Sammie, thank you very much for saving our little Polo from the storm and taking such good care of him. We were so sad last night without him. We live close to the park and your mother said you can come visit and play with Polo and Lin whenever you want."

Sammie was all smiles when she heard this and also from Polo licking her face again because he was so very happy. As the weather turned nicer, Lin and Sammie played with Polo in the park and the "poodle in the puddle" became the "poodle in the middle" of a new friendship.

Edwards Brothers Malloy
Oxnard, CA USA
August 13, 2015